The Puppy without a Tail

THE PUPPY without a Tail

Attilio Guardo

ReadersMagnet, LLC

The Puppy without a Tail
Copyright © 2020 by Attilio Guardo

Published in the United States of America
ISBN Paperback: 978-1-950947-70-6
ISBN eBook: 978-1-950947-71-3

All rights reserved. No part of this publication may be reproduced, stored in a retrieval system or transmitted in any way by any means, electronic, mechanical, photocopy, recording or otherwise without the prior permission of the author except as provided by USA copyright law.

The opinions expressed by the author are not necessarily those of ReadersMagnet, LLC.

ReadersMagnet, LLC
10620 Treena Street, Suite 230 | San Diego, California, 92131 USA
1.619.354.2643 | www.readersmagnet.com

Book design copyright © 2020 by ReadersMagnet, LLC. All rights reserved.
Cover design by Ericka Walker
Interior design by Shemaryl Evans

To my Grandchildren

CHAPTER 1

Jimmy and Jody were excited. Their Beagle had just had five puppies. Now the puppies would need names. It was up to Jimmy and Jody to think of some.

"Let's think of something different," said Jimmy.

"And something funny," answered Jody. They tossed names back and forth, but none of them seemed right.

"How about lollipop?" Jody laughed.

"You meatball," said Jimmy Laughing. "What kind of name is that?"

"That's it," said Jody. "Why don't we name them funny names like Sausage and Hotdog?"

"Okay," agreed Jimmy. "What about the name, Salami?"

"Great, Jimmy. That makes three. Now we need two more."

"I know another one, Hamburg," shouted Jimmy.

"You're a Hamburg brain," laughed Jody.

"Well this Hamburg brain just thought of the fifth name."

"Well, let's hear it," said an anxious Jody.

"You ready for this, dear sister?"

"Yes I am. Come on, let's hear it."

Jimmy raised his arms high above his head. Then he dropped them and pointed at Jody saying, "The name is Porkchop."

Jody laughed hard. "You crack me up, Jimmy. Wait until mom hears our names. I wonder what she will think."

"That they are great, of course. Remember, she said we can name all the puppies."

"I know," Jody replied. "But we are going to sell them. Mom said most of the people who buy them will give them new names."

"Maybe someone will keep one of our fun names," said Jimmy hopefully.

"I sure hope so," answered Jody.

"I know. Maybe mom will let us keep one of Lady's puppies."

"Let's keep the one we named Porkchop," said Jody.

"This is fun, Jody. Let's go see our fun puppies," and the children went to see them.

The Puppy without a Tail

The puppies were all snuggled up to their mother and were all asleep. Jody and Jimmy looked them over. They decided what each one's name would be. There was something different about each one.

Lady was a good and gentle mother. She would always let the children pick up the puppies. Lady new the children loved her and her puppies.

A few days later, Jody noticed a strange thing. One of Lady's puppies did not have a tail. It was the one named Sausage.

"It's true, Jody," said Jimmy. "Sausage doesn't have a tail. not even a little stump. What can we do?"

"There is nothing we can do. "We just won't mention tails in front of him. And we will let Sausage think he has one."

"But what if he wants to wag it?" asked Jimmy.

"How can he wag something he doesn't have?"

"I don't know, Jody. That's why I asked you."

"Well, Jimmy, maybe Sausage's tail is late. Maybe it will start growing in a few days."

"I hope so. He's not going to be very happy when he finds out he has no tail."

Every day Jody and Jimmy checked Sausage. There was no sign of a tail.

"I guess it's no use, Jimmy," Jody said sadly. "I guess he just isn't going to have one, and I don't understand why?"

"Poor, Sausage, how are we going to sell him? No one will want him without a tail."

"Maybe mom will let us keep him. I still love him even though he has no tail," said Jody.

"So do I," Jimmy was quick to answer.

The puppies were getting bigger. Jody and Jimmy noticed how the puppies wagged their tails whenever they played with each other, and when people gave them attention.

One day the puppies were playing together with a ball. They started wagging their tails when they saw Jody and Jimmy.

"Hi, puppies," Jody greeted them. The puppies all gathered around the children with their tails wagging. Then Jody noticed Sausage. His little nose was moving side to side. It was like a wagging tail.

"Look, Jimmy," said Jody excitedly. "Sausage's nose is wiggling and it's acting like a tail. He is so cute."

"I can see it does wiggle. I guess he has a special kind of nose instead of a tail."

"I want to keep him," said Jody.

"You know what mom said. She did not promise we could, just maybe."

"I know," replied Jody. "She also told us not to get too attached to the puppies. I know they will be going to new homes, but darn, I want to keep Sausage."

Said Jimmy, "I'll go get mom so she can see Sausage's nose." A moment later, Jimmy was back with his mother.

"Mom, look at Sausage's nose," said Jody excitedly. "It wiggles."

"Well I'll be, it does," said the children's mother. "I have never seen anything like it before."

"Can we keep him?" begged Jody.

"Now children, you know what we agreed on. I said maybe, and that is how it will be."

"But Sausage is different, and he is so cute. I know you think so too," said Jody.

"Yes, he is different and cute. And he may be sold along with the others," said the children's mother.

Jimmy and Jody knew their mother was serious, but they couldn't stop hoping she somehow would let them keep Sausage.

"Gee, Jimmy," said Jody. "It's hard not to get attached to the puppies. I had no idea I would feel this way. I'm going to feel sad when we sell them."

"I know, Jody, I feel the same way. I don't think I want to be around when they are sold."

"I do," said Jody. "I want to be sure they go to good people and homes, and I want to see the people who buy them."

"I'm going to hate to see Sausage go."

"I don't know if I'll be able to stand it," said Jody, and she picked Sausage up and rocked him in her arms like a baby.

"I know," said Jimmy. "When the people come to buy the puppies we will show them Sausage last."

"Good idea," agreed Jody. Then Jody thought for a minute. But what will we do when all the other puppies are gone? We will have to show sausage then."

"Don't worry, Jody. I'll think of something."

"I sure hope so," and Jody gave a big sigh.

CHAPTER 2

The puppies were now seven weeks old, and the children spent a great deal of time with them. The five puppies were outside most of the time. They would chase bees and butterflies and sniff the flowers. And they chased each other and rolled in the grass.

One day the children left the puppies alone in the yard. It wasn't long before they found their way into the family garden. It was full of all kinds of things for them to play with. Some pulled at the little green tomatoes. Others stepped on top of the radishes and dug holes. Sausage tugged on an eggplant and pulled it out of the ground. He dragged the plant all over the yard. Hamburg took a yellow summer squash and shook it hard. They were all having fun.

It was Jody who first noticed the puppies by the garden. "Wow", she cried. "Jimmy, where

are you? The puppies are in trouble, and so are we I believe."

"I'm here, sister, Jody. What's going on?" he asked with concern.

"Everything," she cried. "The puppies are having a ball tearing up mom's garden."

In a moment Jimmy and Jody were rounding up the puppies, and they could not keep from laughing at them. Hamburg was shaking a summer squash when it flew from his mouth and hit Jimmy on the leg. And Sausage was a humorous sight dragging an eggplant that was larger than him. Sometime later the puppies were rounded up.

"Well, Jody, let's fix things up before mom sees the damage. You stay with the puppies and I'll fill the holes."

"I hope you can save the eggplant. You know how mom loves eggplant," said Jody.

Jimmy laughed as he filled the holes. Then he laughed harder as he planted the eggplant. He could still see Sausage dragging the plant around the yard.

"I guess everything is in order, Jody."

"Good, but what about the green tomatoes and summer squash the puppies removed?" asked Jody.

"I guess we can tell mom we felt like eating green tomatoes and summer squash, so we picked some."

"I would rather be punished than tell mom that," said Jody.

"Me too," said Jimmy reconsidering. "Anyway, I was only joking. I think mom will understand. Let's tell her."

"Look mom," said Jimmy and Jody together. "Look what the puppies picked from the garden."

"I see, children, little green tomatoes and summer squash. How nice, and I hope you children like them. You can have them for supper."

"Sure, mom, we'll eat them," said Jody.

"Should I dare ask what else the puppies did to my garden?"

Jimmy and Jody looked at each other. Then Jimmy spoke. "Well, they did dig a few holes and Sausage dragged an eggplant around the yard. But I fixed everything, mom, just like before."

"I see, I guess puppies will be puppies. And I see my children don't always watch the puppies."

"We'll be more careful, mom." They won't get into the garden again," promised Jody.

"Anyway, children, I placed an ad in the newspaper. People will be coming to buy the puppies soon."

The next morning a big man and a little boy came to buy a puppy. "I'm Mr. Carey," he said in a loud voice. "This is my son Tommy, and he wants a puppy."

Jimmy and Jody stared at the big man with the dark beard. The little boy looked so tiny next to him.

"The puppies are in the garage, Mr. Carey. Come and choose the one you want," said the children's mother.

"Which one do you want?" The big man asked his little boy. The little boy looked at the puppies. Then he pointed to Sausage and said, "I want that one."

"Oh, you don't want him," said Jimmy. "He was born last and still needs his mother."

"Wait a minute," said the big man. "That puppy has no tail. We'll take another one," and he pointed to Hamburg.

"That is Hamburg," said Jimmy. The big man laughed loudly and said, "Hamburg, that's some name."

Jody looked at the big man. Then she asked, "Will you give Hamburg a good home?"

"Sure, little lady. We sure will, and I promise we won't eat him," Joked the big man. "You can come visit him whenever you want."

"That is nice of you, Mr. Carey," said the children's mother. Jody and Jimmy watched in silence as the big man picked up Hamburg.

"Don't you worry. We'll take good care of him. Thank you folks," he said, and he and the little boy left. And Hamburg was gone. Jody started sobbing and softly said "I'll miss him."

"Me too," said Jimmy.

"Letting the first one go is always the hardest," said the children's mother. "I'm sure Mr. Carey and his boy will give Hamburg a lot of love."

"I sure hope so," said Jimmy.

CHAPTER 3

The next morning two older ladies came to buy a puppy. "We are sisters, and we want to buy two puppies that are also sisters."

"Children, go get the puppies," commanded their mother. Jody and Jimmie returned with the four puppies.

"Oh my, what adorable puppies," said the ladies.

"Those two are sisters," said Jody pointing. "Hotdog is the one tugging on your laces and the other one is Salami."

"What funny names," laughed the two ladies. "Will it make you happy if we keep the same names?"

"Yes," said Jody quickly. The children liked the two older ladies, and each sister picked up a puppy.

"We will see to it that they are always happy," the sisters promised.

"That's neat," said Jimmy.

"I'm glad Hotdog and Salami can be together," said Jody.

"When the puppies get older we will stop by for a visit. I'm sure you would like that. This way you can see how the puppies have grown," said one of the ladies.

"That will be great," said Jimmy and Jody together. The children said goodbye to Hotdog and Salami, and the ladies left.

"I am going to miss them," said Jody. "I knew we couldn't keep them all, but I feel sad when they are sold."

"I know. All we have left is Porkchop and Sausage," said Jimmy sadly.

"Somehow we must keep Sausage," said Jody.

Later that day, a thin man with eyeglasses came to buy a puppy. "I am Mr. Tibbs, and I want to surprise my children with a puppy."

"We have two left," said the children's mother. The thin man looked the puppies over. He petted and talked to them. Then he said," That one has no tail. Did something happen to him?"

"No," said Jimmy. "He was born that way."

"I see," said the man. "I guess I'll take the other one."

"We call him Porkchop," said Jody. "Will you give him a good home?"

"Oh yes," answered the man. "We had our other dog fifteen years. I'll certainly give him a good home."

The children smiled at the man and the man smiled back. He picked up Porkchop and said, "Thank you folks and I'll be going now."

Jimmy and Jody watched until he drove away. All the puppies were now gone except Sausage. The children missed them more now.

"It seems so strange without them," said Jody.

"Why don't we talk to mom now about Sausage," said Jimmy. "Maybe she will let us keep him."

The children found their mother and asked her, "May we keep Sausage now?"

"Let's see what happens tomorrow, for that will be the last day of the ad," she said.

Until tomorrow thought Jimmy and Jody, for it would decide if Sausage was to be theirs. Oh, how they wanted him. No one must come to buy him, wished Jody. Not a single soul.

Later that night, the children went to bed. All Jody could think about was Sausage. She closed her eyes and soon fell asleep and slipped into a dream.

In her dream she could see Sausage as if she was there with him, but he could not see her. Then she could see a women and a young boy buying him, and taking her Sausage away. "No," she sobbed and cried," bring him back," but they did not hear her.

CHAPTER 4

In her dream, the young boy threw a stick and said, "Go get it, Sausage." The puppy chewed on the stick as he ran around the boy. "Bring it here," the little boy called again, and the puppy did.

"Good boy, Sausage," and the boy petted him. Sausage's nose was moving side to side.

"So you don't have a tail," said the young boy, "but you have a special nose that can smell things a mile away and can wiggle side to side. I love you, Sausage," said the young boy, and the puppy licked him on the face. The two played and played together, and it was a beautiful sight to see. The boy loved his dog more than anything he ever had.

"My friends must see my dog," the young boy said. "They must see his special nose." So the young boy called two of his friends over to see his dog.

They looked at Sausage and said, "What happened to his tail?" They laughed and said, "Who ever heard of a dog without a tail. Why don't you pin one on him?" and they laughed some more.

"Stop," The young boy shouted. "He may not have a tail, but he has a very special nose. See, it wiggles side to side."

"Who cares," they cried. "Even his nose is strange. I'm glad he isn't our dog."

The young boy was sad. "I thought you were my friends," he said. "You are cruel to make fun of my puppy. He will grow up to be a smart dog. You will see."

"Let's go," said the young boy's friends. "Let's go and play with a real dog," and they walked away.

The young boy picked up his puppy and said, "Don't worry, I'll never give you up and I'll always want you. I don't care what other people say."

Later, a group of children came in the young boy's yard. "Let us see your dog without a tail. We hear he is really funny looking," said one of the children.

The young boy took the puppy in his arms and said, "Why should you care? He is my dog and you can't look at him."

"Yes we can. You can't hide him all of the time," said some of the children.

The young boy knew they were right, and it made him sad. He wondered when they would stop laughing at his puppy. "Go home, and you are not welcome here," he told the children. Then he went into the house.

Sausage could see the young boy was sad. And the puppy knew it was because he had no tail. Sausage loved the young boy as the young boy loved him, so Sausage decided he would run away and find a tail. When he found one, he would come back to the young boy. The next day, early the next morning Sausage started on his journey. As he walked along he met a black poodle.

"Where are you going," asked the poodle.

"I am going to find a tail," answered Sausage. "My master loves me, but all the children make fun of me because I have no tail. This makes my master sad."

"I see," said the poodle. "Maybe I can help you."

"You can?" said Sausage excitedly.

"Yes," answered the poodle, "but you must journey far to the next town. Then you must cross the fields and the stream of water at the foot of the mountain. Then you must find the Great White German Shepherd. She will help you."

"Then I will go," said Sausage full of hope.

"It won't be an easy journey," said the black poodle.

"Because I love my master, I will go."

"Good luck," said the poodle, and Sausage continued on his journey.

He walked and he walked and he walked. He had never walked so much in one day. His little paws were tired and aching. He was also thirsty and warm from the hot sun. And now he was feeling hungry. He thought about food and where would he get it. Then he thought of the young boy giving him food, but now he was alone and there would be no food.

"Because I love my master, I will go without food," Sausage convinced himself. "I must find a tail. That is more important. I must make my master happy."

Sausage continued walking. He walked until the hot sun was no longer shinning. *"I must find a place to sleep,"* he thought. Then he thought of his bed the young boy had gotten for him. He

The Puppy without a Tail

wished he could sleep in it now. He was so tired and hungry.

Sausage lifted his nose and sifted the air. He could smell hay and dry wood, and what he smelled was a barn that was nearby. It was not long before Sausage came upon the barn. It was very old and was leaning to one side. *"I will find some hay and fall asleep, and I will continue my journey tomorrow,"* thought Sausage. He saw some hay in the corner of the barn, and when he was about to lie on the hay a large raccoon jumped at him from out of the darkness. The raccoon struck Sausage on the face with his paw knocking him over. When Sausage got up the raccoon jumped on his back and bit him. The pain was intense and made Sausage yelp. Somehow, he managed to free himself from the raccoon and ran out of the barn. His face was scratched and cut.

How he wished the young boy was with him. He knew his master would take care of him and make the pain go away. And he did not understand why the raccoon had attacked him.

Sausage walked until he came to an old tree stump with a small cavity. *"I will sleep here,"* he decided, and he curled up in the cavity. He was so tired he quickly fell asleep. He was not asleep long when rain drops started falling upon his fur waking him. A moment later, lighting started to light up the sky. It was followed by loud thunder. At times the thunder was so loud it made the ground shake. It frightened sausage and made his little body tremble. A wind was now blowing in the direction of the cavity causing his fur to become wet. It made him cold and he started to shiver. *"Where can I go,"* he thought. *"If only I could find a tail. Then I could go back to my master."*

Sausage was shivering harder, and his fur was very wet from the cold rain. *"Where can I go,"* he again thought. Then he knew there was nowhere. He curled up in the small stump as the rain came down harder.

CHAPTER 5

It was morning and the sun was shining. Sausage shook and shook the water from his fur. The warm sun felt good on him and he knew it would soon dry his body. He was hungry, but he had to continue his journey. His love for the young boy was stronger than ever. He just had to find the Great White Shepherd. She would give him a tail so he could go back to his master. Then they would be happy.

As Sausage started to walk, his back and feet ached, but he continued his journey. Several times along the way he sneezed. The rain had irritated his nostrils. Finally he came to the large fields. There was tall green grass and pretty colored wild flowers. Sausage remembered what the black poodle had said. There would be the fields and the stream of water at the foot of the mountains.

As tired as Sausage was, he started running through the fields toward the mountains. He was running when he suddenly stepped on a nest of bees. He felt a sting on his paw. Then he felt another and another. He ran and ran until the bees were gone. Finally he stopped and licked were the bees had stung him. Sausage was tired, and so he rested. He did not want to walk anymore. The bees had hurt him and he felt weak. "But because I love my master, I must go on," he thought.

And Sausage did. He walked and walked until he came to the stream of water. The water was cold and it was moving swiftly. He had to cross it to get to the foot of the mountain. Sausage looked at the water and walked back and forth. Then he thought of the young boy and the Great White Shepherd. Seconds later he scratched at the ground with his paw and then plunged into the water.

The water was moving swiftly and started to carry him away. He paddled quickly with his paws and kept his head above the water, but it was still carrying him away. Sausage paddled harder and harder, and with great determination he finally reached the other side of the stream. When he reached the land, he lay on the ground and closed his eyes. He could not take another step. His strength was gone.

Sausage lay there for a long time. When he opened his eyes, he could see a bright light. In the center of the light was the Great White Shepherd. She was large and beautiful, and her fur was as white as snow. Sausage could see there was something magical about her.

"So you are Sausage," said the shepherd. "You have had a hard journey. What is it that you want?" Sausage could not believe he had found her. He was tired and weak and did not believe his eyes. "I have no tail," said Sausage. "I left my master so I could find one. Everyone makes fun of me and it makes my master sad. If I have a tail my master won't be sad anymore."

"I see," said the shepherd. "Is this the only reason you came to see me?"

"Yes," answered Sausage. "The black poodle I met said you would help me."

"Does your master love you?" asked the shepherd.

"Oh yes, very much," answered Sausage.

"And do you love your master?" asked the shepherd.

"Oh yes, very much."

"You have journeyed far and proven your love for your master. You are lucky to have each other and such a strong love."

"Yes, I know," said Sausage.

The Great White Shepherd was silent as she looked at Sausage. Then she spoke. "You having a tail won't make your master love you anymore than he does now. We are what we are. Do you not have a very special nose?" asked the shepherd.

"Oh yes, I know," said Sausage.

"And you don't have to look beyond it to find happiness," said the shepherd. "Your master loves you just the way you are."

"But what about the other people who don't?" asked Sausage.

"In time they will understand," said the shepherd. "Remember, there are several dogs with tails that don't have the love your master gives you. Go back to your master as you are."

"I will," said Sausage. "I miss my master very much."

"If you close your eyes," said the shepherd, "I will return you to your master in an instant. I will touch you with my paw and your journey will be over."

Sausage closed his eyes and he felt the paw of the Great White Shepherd upon him.

CHAPTER 6

"Wake up, Jody, you are dreaming," Jimmy was saying, and he had his hand on her shoulder.

Jody opened her eyes and said, "The Great White Shepherd is touching me." "The what?" asked Jimmy.

"I guess I was dreaming," said Jody. "I was dreaming about Sausage."

"It must have been pretty real."

"Oh, how real it was," said Jody.

"Please tell me about it," pleaded Jimmy.

"I will. I want to tell you and mom all about it."

And Jody did. She told them all about her amazing dream.

"That was some dream, Jody," said the children's mother.

"Can we keep Sausage, mom?" begged the children. "We don't want him running away like the dream."

"You can keep him," said the children's mother.

"We can?" said Jimmy and Jody excitedly.

"Yes, you can."

"Thanks, mom, we love you," and the children hugged her strongly.

A moment later, Jody asked, "Where is sausage?"

"I let him out in the backyard a little while ago," Jimmy informed her.

Jody ran to the window that faced the backyard and looked out.

"Oh my," she shouted. "There is a Great White Shepherd in the yard with Sausage. I better go get Sausage before he gets hurt." Jody ran outside and when she reached Sausage the Great White Shepherd was gone.

She looked at Sausage and his little nose was wiggling side to side.

www.ingramcontent.com/pod-product-compliance
Lightning Source LLC
LaVergne TN
LVHW050138080526
838202LV00061B/6530